FATHER CHRISTMAS
HEARD A PARP

For Tuesday and Cissy

First published in paperback in Great Britain by HarperCollins *Children's Books* in 2017

1 3 5 7 9 10 8 6 4 2

ISBN: 978-0-00-824152-0

HarperCollins *Children's Books* is a division of HarperCollins *Publishers* Ltd.

Text and illustrations copyright © Olaf Falafel 2017

Visit our website at www.harpercollins.co.uk

Printed and bound in China

FATHER CHRISTMAS HEARD A PARP

Olaf Falafel

HarperCollins *Children's Books*

Father Christmas heard a parp...
E-I-E-I-O!

He thought that parp came from a bird ...
E - I - E - I - O!

Father Christmas heard a parp...
E-I-E-I-O!

Father Christmas
heard a parp...
E-I-E-I-O!

He thought that parp
came from Rodney...
E-I-E-I-O!

Father Christmas
heard a parp...
E-I-E-I-O!

He thought that parp
came from an elf ...
E-I-E-I-O!

Father Christmas heard a parp...
E-I-E-I-O!

He thought that parp came from a choir...
E-I-E-I-O!

Here a **Thrrbb**

there a **Blrlrlr**

everywhere a **Bwwb Bwwb**

Father Christmas heard a parp...
E - I - E - I - O!

Father Christmas
heard a parp...
E-I-E-I-O!

Turns out that parp came from...

...a TREE?

rang the sound of a parp...

...from an overfed mouse!